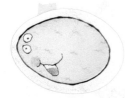

Attack of the Mutants

A  Adventure

by Ann Hodgman

illustrated by Mones

adapted from the teleplay
by Julian P. Gardner

Random House 🏠 New York

Library of Congress Cataloging in Publication Data: Hodgman, Ann. Attack of the Mutants. SUMMARY: Established in Cats' Lair, their fortress on Third Earth, the six Thundercats find themselves in grave danger when their headquarters is infiltrated by enemy Mutants. 1. Children's stories, American. [1. Science fiction] I. Mones, ill. II. Title. PZ7.H6648At   1985   [Fic] 85-2015   ISBN: 0-394-87452-8

THUNDERCATS and THUNDERCATS characters are trademarks of Telepictures Corporation.

Manufactured in the United States of America   1 2 3 4 5 6 7 8 9 0

It was a clear, sunny morning on Third Earth.

Above the green meadows loomed the Cats' Lair, mighty castle of the Thundercats. Slowly its huge stone head turned from left to right, as if surveying for intruders, while dazzling electron beams shot from its eyes. A living fortress, it was alert to any sign of danger in that peaceful landscape.

This was the home the Thundercats had built on Third Earth when their own planet, Thundera, had been destroyed. Their band had six members: Lion-O, the Thundercats' youthful leader; Cheetara, who was swifter than any cheetah; Tygra, a master of camouflage, who was able to blend into any background; Panthro, an acrobat and martial artist; and the prankish Wilykit and Wilykat, whose repertoire of practical jokes could disarm any enemy.

And then there was Snarf, Lion-O's faithful guardian—a space sheepdog who would never believe that Lion-O could take care of himself.

The Thundercats had to be on constant guard against their many enemies. S-S-Slithe, a Mutant reptile, lived in Castle Plun-Darr with his fellow Mutants. Mumm-Ra, a loathsome mummy-being who had lived for seven thousand years, ruled his evil domain from the fearsome Black Pyramid. Though they distrusted each other, S-S-Slithe and Mumm-Ra had a common bond—their deep hatred of the Thundercats. It was their goal to possess the Eye of Thundera, the source of the Thundercats' power. And they never ceased trying.

Inside the Cat's Head, Tygra and Panthro were running a test of the lair's intricate defense system.

Tygra studied the graph console. "Let's try the enlarger, Panthro," he said.

Panthro punched a button. Instantly the image of a volcano jumped onto the telescreen in front of him. A blur was racing around its base.

It was Cheetara, out for her morning jog.

"Incredible," said Tygra. "I clock her at a 30-second mile."

He switched off the telescreen. "Let's go get some exercise ourselves."

If they had stayed to watch the telescreen, they would have seen that Cheetara's astonishing pace was slowing . . . and slowing . . . and finally stopping. She was in trouble! She looked around in bewilderment, took a few more steps—and fell to the ground.

Two of S-S-Slithe's Mutant henchmen were watching.

Chittering with excitement, a Monkian scuttled over to Cheetara's unconscious form. A Jackalman loped along behind him, panting. Leering, they picked up the tiny blowdart that had felled her. Then they pulled Cheetara onto a stretcher and carried her away into the underbrush.

A little later, at Castle Plun-Darr, S-S-Slithe interrogated them.

"Did you get her? Yes-s-s?" he asked eagerly, rubbing his scaly hands in anticipation.

"Yes, of course we got her!" squealed the Monkian indignantly. "She's *there* now!"

"I hope this works," said S-S-Slithe. "Those cats-s-s are very clever . . . and I don't trust Mumm-Ra. But it *is* a good plan. So we'll wait . . . and s-s-see. Yes-s-s?"

"Yes-s-s," the Monkian and Jackalman replied in unison.

▼   ▼   ▼

Thunder crashed in the stormy sky above the Black Pyramid, Mumm-Ra's stronghold. Around its polished onyx sides stretched miles of bleak and barren desert. Beyond the desert was the Field of Daggers. Only the most determined traveler could reach the Black Pyramid. And Cheetara was trapped inside.

She lay unconscious on a stone slab in Mumm-Ra's Tomb Room. Wrapped in decaying bandages, Mumm-Ra walked around her, gloating. Only his evil eyes could be seen, and they flashed triumphantly.

"So the cheetah has been trapped," he sneered. "Cheetara, they call you—the quick. We were not quite so quick this time, were

9

we? But fear not, fast one. You shall be back among your friends this very night . . . and you will remember none of this. Sleep—and dream peaceful dreams while Mumm-Ra calls upon all of his strength to leave this pyramid in a new form he has never assumed before. Behold!''

He stretched his arms heavenward. Around him, the room took on a sinister glow. Mumm-Ra began to chant.

''Ancient spirits of evil . . . transform this ancient body into Pumm-Ra, the Puma of Thundera!''

The statues in the room glimmered with an eerie light. Sheets of lightning crackled through the air. The transformation was beginning.

A swirl of smoke filled the room. When it cleared, Mumm-Ra had taken on a new form. The decaying mummy was gone. Now he looked like a lithe, handsome puma—like a Thundercat!

He paused a moment to savor his new shape. Then, grinning, he lifted Cheetara off the slab and carried her out of the room.

Cheetara blinked. Startled, she looked around.

''Drink this,'' came a gentle voice. ''It will make you feel better.''

Cheetara saw a handsome, catlike man kneeling next to her.

''What—what happened? Who are you?'' she asked.

The man spoke soothingly. ''You were captured by some strange creature. I heard the name. It was Smythe, I think.''

''S-S-Slithe!'' Cheetara gasped.

''Yes, that could be it. They drugged you. They were about to carry you away when I appeared. I fought them off. I am pleased that you seem to be well, and so I shall be on my way . . .''

He knew Cheetara wouldn't let him leave.

She didn't. "Wait," she said urgently. "Who are you? You look strangely familiar—like someone I have known in the past. Are you from this Third Earth?"

"No," Mumm-Ra answered. "I am Pumm-Ra. I come from a distant planet called—"

"Thundera!" Cheetara cried.

Pumm-Ra seemed surprised. "You know Thundera?"

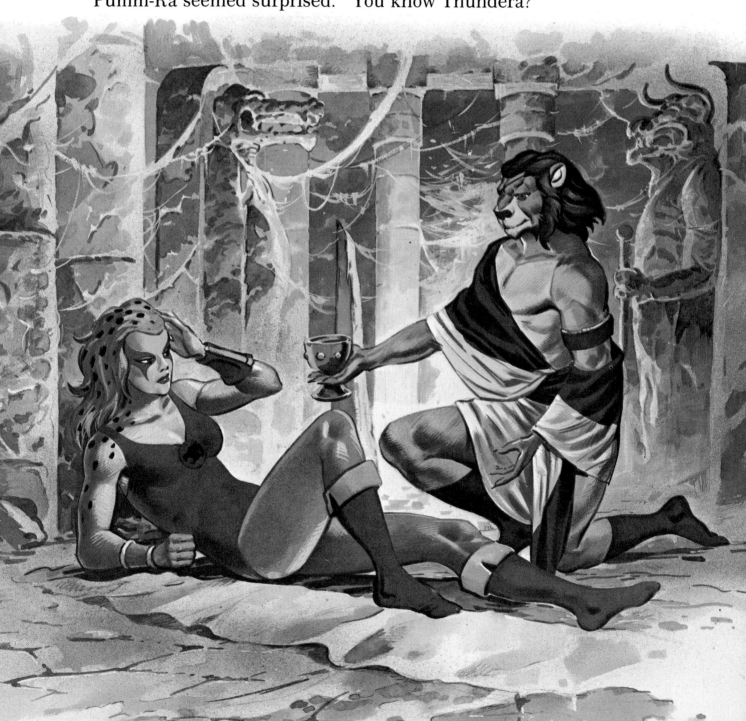

"It is—it was—my home. You must come with me to the Cats' Lair and meet my friends, the Thundercats!"

"I would like that," Pumm-Ra said. He smiled. "Yes, I would like that very much."

An hour later the Thundercats were talking with their new friend. All were grateful to Pumm-Ra for rescuing Cheetara.

As leader of the Thundercats, it was up to Lion-O to thank him.

"Pumm-Ra," he said, "we owe you so much for saving Cheetara's life. Our home is open to you for as long as you would like to stay."

"You have my deep gratitude for this kindness," said Pumm-Ra, bowing slightly. "I look forward to many happy days amongst you. And now, if you will excuse me, I will retire." He smiled at the group. "Until morning," he said, and left the room.

For a moment no one spoke. Then Snarf broke the silence. "I don't trust him!"

"Snarf, Snarf, why do you say that? You don't even *know* him!" answered Lion-O indulgently. He was used to Snarf's fussing.

Snarf looked sheepish, but he was determined. "Just a Snarf's intuition, that's all."

Cheetara gave Snarf an affectionate smile. "Still the same old worrier," she said. "But you'd be a lot more worried if he hadn't rescued me, you know. I'm certainly glad he came along."

"So am I," said Panthro. "Perhaps we should ask him to join us."

"Good idea," said Tygra. "What do the rest of you think?"

▼   ▼   ▼

Pumm-Ra wasn't wasting any time as the Thundercats talked. In his guest room, he was improvising a headset. He put on the earphones, stuck the aerial out his window, and whispered cautiously into the microphone.

"Do you hear me? S-S-Slithe . . . are you there, Reptilian?" he murmured.

The radio crackled for a second. Then came S-S-Slithe's answering hiss. "Yes-s-s, we are here—and we are prepared. Where are you?"

"Where I am supposed to be!" said Pumm-Ra smugly. "In the Cats' Lair, of course."

S-S-Slithe hissed approvingly. "We must know what their plans are," he said. "If you can find their war room—"

Pumm-Ra cut him off. "Mumm-Ra—I mean Pumm-Ra—does not need any instructions," he said curtly. "Just be sure you are where you are supposed to be at high noon tomorrow."

"Yes-s-s, we will certainly be there," answered S-S-Slithe.

▼　　　▼　　　▼

Back in the Council Chamber Room, the Thundercats were still discussing their new companion.

"This puma has apparently saved Cheetara's life," said Tygra, "and he appears to be one of us. Have you anything more to say about him, Cheetara?" he asked. "You didn't actually see him before you fainted, did you?"

"No—no, that's true," said Cheetara. "But when I awoke—"

"I vote we take him in!" Lion-O said eagerly.

But as he spoke, the misty image of Jaga the Wise—the Thundercats' legendary commander—materialized in front of him, and Jaga's voice echoed in the air.

"Be not hasty, Lion-O," Jaga cautioned. "One does not make

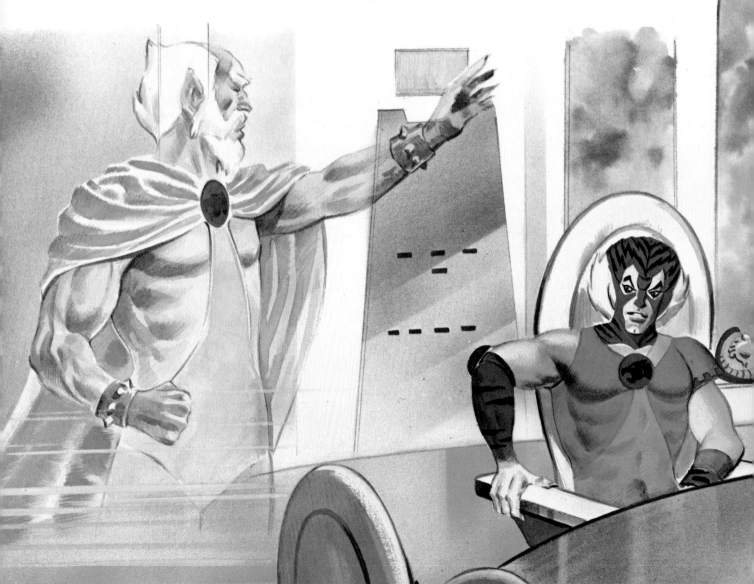

decisions by instinct alone. Let the facts weigh heavily on your mind. And listen to your peers!''

Lion-O looked abashed. "You are right, Jaga,'' he said. "I should take more time in making important decisions. Tygra, how will *you* vote?''

"I vote to give the puma a week's probation,'' said Tygra.

"I agree,'' said Panthro. "If he is who he seems to be, he should have no objections.''

Cheetara thought for a minute. "I suppose we cannot ask him to join us until we know we can trust him,'' she said at last.

"So say you all?'' asked Tygra.

They spoke in unison. "By the Code of Thundera!''

Alone in his room that night, Pumm-Ra stole to the door and listened.

"They must all be asleep by now," he decided. "And while the Thundercats sleep, Pumm-Ra works!"

And he went to work—his own special kind of work. First he unplugged all the telescreens and jammed the lair's communications systems. He readjusted the Cat's Head motor and the drawbridge controls to suit his own purposes. He rewired the ThunderTank so that none but he and his allies could drive it.

Then he stole into the weapons room, where all the Thundercats' weapons were stored. But where was Lion-O's Sword—the Sword containing the Eye of Thundera? It was nowhere to be seen.

"Drat," Pumm-Ra muttered. "It must be in Lion-O's room."

He tiptoed down the hall to check, but the Sword was not there. Pumm-Ra strode angrily away. Then he stopped and turned around.

He had noticed a door in the wall. It had no handle.

Pumm-Ra laughed a quiet, sinister laugh.

"Yes," he sneered, "this door would be safely locked to anyone but Mumm-Ra. They have used an old Egyptian tomb device, unknown for thousands of years—unknown, that is, *except* to one who has *lived* for thousands of years."

He gave one stone a gentle turn . . . and the door slid open.

In the middle of the Sword Chamber, under a soft light, was the Mystic Sword of Omens.

Pumm-Ra reached for it.

From the Sword's hilt the Eye of Thundera gave a low growl.

He reached for it again. Again the Eye growled.

Pumm-Ra stretched his hand out yet again. This time, though,

he reached for the Eye instead of the Sword's handle. Swiftly he clapped his hand over the Eye. It gave a muffled roar, but Pumm-Ra was ready now. He wrapped the Eye tightly in a cloth.

"That will keep it quiet," he said with satisfaction. Then he examined it. "Strange," he said. "The Sword is much smaller than when I last saw it!"

Pumm-Ra did not know that the Sword could reach its full length—and its full power—only in the hand of its proper owner, Lion-O.

He tapped the Sword lightly, almost affectionately. "Well, no matter," he said. "It is *mine*. Details can come later!"

▼   ▼   ▼

Of course Pumm-Ra mentioned nothing about this the next morning in the Thundercats' Council Chamber Room.

"I understand your decision, and I agree with it," he said. "I hope I will prove worthy of your trust."

Snarf muttered suspiciously to himself. Everyone ignored him.

"We hope so too," said Tygra.

Panthro stood up. "Come on, Tygra, Cheetara. We have work to do in the Thundrillium Fields."

"Are you going to take the ThunderTank?" Lion-O asked.

Pumm-Ra froze. If they took the tank, they'd find out he'd sabotaged it!

"No, not today," answered Panthro. "We'll walk."

Pumm-Ra relaxed again. Everything was going according to plan.

"Lion-O, we'll be back at noon," Panthro said, and they set out for the fields.

A few minutes before noon Lion-O and Snarf were playing a game of ring-toss, Snarf-style: Snarf pointed his furry tail straight into the air and Lion-O tossed the rings onto it. Lion-O had won so many games that Snarf was getting restless.

"This game is beginning to bore me," he complained. "I mean *my* part in it is."

"Well, guarding this place is just as boring," Lion-O answered. "Who'd be fool enough to attack this fortress? It's invulnerable. Let's go and have a look through the Cat's Eyes and see how Panthro and the group are making out. They should be back any minute."

They walked into the Cat's Head control room. Lion-O sat down at the control console.

He pushed the "on" button for the left eye. Nothing happened.

He pushed the "on" button for the right eye. Nothing happened.

He pulled the "on" switch for the telescreen. Nothing.

"Strange. . . . Maybe the master power supply is malfunctioning," said Lion-O.

But the power supply was working.

"Something's really wrong here," said Snarf.

For once Lion-O didn't laugh at him. "Yes, this is serious," he agreed. "I'd better use the Sword to see where Panthro is."

He sprang to his feet and went to the Sword Chamber, with Snarf at his heels.

The Sword was gone.

Now Lion-O and Snarf were really worried. "You'd better call them on the corresponder in the ThunderTank," said Snarf. "That is, if *it's* working!"

But it wasn't. And the ThunderTank only coughed and went dead when Lion-O tried to start it.

"This is trouble, Snarf," said Lion-O grimly. "*Big* trouble."

The Mutants were watching the Cats' Lair from a spot nearby. As they watched, the Cat's Eyes began to blink in code.

It was Pumm-Ra's signal to them.

"Good," said S-S-Slithe. "S-s-somehow he has done it. The Cats' Lair is as good as ours."

And they chortled with Mutant glee.

Lion-O and Snarf were heading back to the lair. They didn't notice Pumm-Ra until they were almost at the door.

He was standing in the doorway. In his hand was the Sword. He lifted it high in the air and waved it tauntingly at them. His laugh was cruel and full of menace.

"I knew it! I just knew it!" moaned Snarf.

Pumm-Ra drew himself up to his full height. "Stand back and do as I say, *boy*," he jeered at Lion-O.

"Who are you?" asked Lion-O fiercely. "You're not from Thundera. What do you want of us?"

Pumm-Ra smiled. "Everything," he said. "I want it all, and before this day is done I shall have it."

"The Sword won't obey you!" shouted Lion-O. "And without it you are no match for me!" He made a rush for the Sword.

Pumm-Ra stepped nimbly out of the way. "Hold!" he cried.

"Your brain speaks faster than your tongue can think! Hold—and be-hold!"

He unwrapped the cloth from the Sword and screamed out the Thundercats' magic incantation: "Thunder-Thunder-Thunder-Thundercats—Ho!"

The sky turned black. Lightning ripped the air. Deafening thunder roared and the wind shrieked. Pumm-Ra's evil was tearing the heavens apart.

As the storm began, the other Thundercats were struggling to reach the lair. "I have never seen the likes of such a storm!" shouted Tygra. His words were almost lost in the howling wind.

"Nature alone could not create such a storm!" said Cheetara. "I sense some other force at work—an evil force!"

"Then we must hurry!" Panthro shouted through the thunder. "The others may need us!"

His eyes were glowing fire. So were the eyes of the other Thundercats. Their special powers were taking hold.

The Thundercats raced toward their lair.

They reached it just in time to see a bolt of jagged lightning striking the Sword in Pumm-Ra's hand. Like a living thing the Sword

sprang from his grip and landed between him and Lion-O. It pulsed with a fiery light.

Jaga's image appeared in the dark sky. His words floated over the sounds of the storm. . . .

"The Mystic Sword of Omens cannot be used for evil deeds," he said. "Attempt it—and know the wrath of Jaga!"

Pumm-Ra ignored him.

Lion-O hurled himself at the Sword. Just as quickly, Pumm-Ra reached for it himself—but Snarf was even quicker. He coiled his long tail around Pumm-Ra's legs and sent him sprawling!

Now Lion-O grabbed the Sword. But Pumm-Ra only laughed disdainfully. "Look behind you!" he sneered. "It's too late, boy!"

23

The Mutants were advancing in the ThunderTank, and its laser guns were firing.

At the same time, Panthro, Tygra, and Cheetara came into view, racing for the Cats' Lair. The Mutants were ready for them—or so they thought. S-S-Slithe turned the laser on his opponents.

He shouldn't have bothered.

Cheetara merely stepped out of the beam's way—in half a millisecond. Tygra dematerialized, and the beam passed harmlessly through the spot where he'd been. And Panthro leaped into a tree in an effortless panther-bound.

As his friends dodged the beam, Lion-O stepped forward to the ThunderTank. Sword in hand, he lopped off the laser beam.

Panthro grabbed the wheel of the ThunderTank and spun it wildly, hurling the Mutants into the air.

"Sorry about that," said Panthro, dusting off his hands.

"Into the Cats' Lair!" screamed Pumm-Ra. He and the Mutants bolted into the lair—and locked the door behind them.

The Thundercats had won round one. But they had lost control of their fortress.

Lion-O sighed. "Well, that takes care of the Mutants—for a while, anyway. But that puma's locked up our lair!"

"Not necessarily," said Tygra.

Panthro looked warily at him. "There's another way in you haven't told us about?"

"Yes," answered Tygra. "Through the power exhaust."

"But suppose he turns the power on?" asked Cheetara.

"It's a chance we'll have to take!" Lion-O said impetuously. "I'll go."

Tygra shook his head. "Lion-O, I'm the architect of the Cats' Lair. I know every turn, nook, and cranny of the system."

"But *I* have the Sword!" argued Lion-O.

As always when Lion-O needed a lesson, Jaga's image appeared.

"Ingenuity is called for here—not bravery and strength," he said gravely. "It is Tygra who should go."

Lion-O swallowed his disappointment and stepped forward to shake his friend's hand. "Good luck, Tygra," he said.

A few seconds later Tygra was deep in the lower reaches of the lair, in the pipeline that led to the fuel room. Once the pipe creaked ominously, but no one seemed to hear it. He crept forward with agonizing slowness, hoping beyond hope that he'd make it out of the pipeline before the power was turned on.

Outside, the other Thundercats waited. Suddenly there was a roar of flame, and then an ominous humming.

Someone had turned on the power!

Then came an even more frightening sound. The Cat's Eyes were turning to focus on them. Someone inside the lair was watching the Thundercats!

"Get out of the sight of those eyes!" commanded Panthro. "And pray that Tygra made it. I'm going to see if he needs a hand."

And before the eyes could spot him, he'd begun to scale the side of the Cats' Lair.

"I'll distract the eyes while he's climbing," said Cheetara, running in a dizzying circle in front of them.

But Lion-O had an even more daring plan. He raised the Sword again.

"Thunder-Thunder-Thunder-Thundercats—Ho!" he cried.

The Sword tripled in length. Its magical Eye shot into the sky. The eyes of the Cat's Head swiveled to focus on it . . . and shattered into thousands of pieces as the Eye roared in fury. The lair door opened, and Lion-O raced inside.

"Wait for Snarf!" Snarf called plaintively. He made it inside just in time before the door crashed shut.

The noise alerted Pumm-Ra. He rushed to a window and caught

sight of Panthro scaling the wall outside. Pumm-Ra cursed in rage.
Then he leaned out and howled an evil charm.

"Spirits of evil . . . send forth an evil force!"

There was an explosion in the sky, and a horrifying kite-monster
swooped down toward Panthro, breathing fire.

With one catlike movement, Panthro flung a chain around its
neck and the monster fell shrieking to the ground. As it fell, its own
fiery breath set it ablaze.

Panthro continued on his way.

Meanwhile, Pumm-Ra was feverishly working the controls inside the Cat's Head. Suddenly he heard a little sound in back of him. Pumm-Ra whirled around, but there was no one there.

At least he didn't *see* anyone there. But Tygra had made it through the power exhaust. Now he'd made himself invisible and come to play.

Tygra's eyes shone in one corner of the room. Then his foot appeared on the other side. He tweaked Pumm-Ra's ear. Then he grabbed Pumm-Ra by the feet and turned him upside down. Pumm-Ra screamed in rage—but he was powerless against his invisible opponent.

"Hold!" Lion-O cried, charging into the room. Behind him were Cheetara and Snarf.

Tygra materialized, and the Thundercats stood looking at their captive.

"It's over, Pumm-Ra," Lion-O said quietly. "You can't defeat us all."

"Who are you?" asked Panthro.

"*What* are you?" asked Cheetara.

Pumm-Ra preened proudly in front of them. "Who am I? Suffice it to say that I have lived for seven thousand years. . . ."

His voice was growing louder and more hollow.

"*I* am not the intruder. It is you who have disturbed *my* rest. But I have time. A thousand years more . . . five thousand . . ."

Before their shocked eyes, the puma was taking on Mumm-Ra's loathsome shape.

"You cannot defeat me, for I am Mumm-Ra. And wherever evil exists, Mumm-Ra lives! Mumm-Ra lives! *Mumm-Ra lives!*"

Mumm-Ra waved a clawed hand—and disappeared.

The Thundercats stared at one another in horror.

"I hope we never see *him* again!" said Snarf with a shudder.

"But you know we will," said Lion-O. He shook his head. "I can't believe I misjudged Pumm-Ra the way I did. I guess new friends aren't as easily made as I thought!"

Cheetara smiled. "But friends like the Thundercats are forever," she said.

They all joined hands.

"Thundercats . . . *forever!*" they said as one.

Mumm-Ra

S-S-Slithe

Monkian

Jackalman